Rachel Woolley
6/29/20

The Victims of

Dr. Pold

The Victims of

Dr. Pold

WRITTEN & ILLUSTRATED
BY
RACHEL WOOLSEY

Charleston, AR:
COBB PUBLISHING
2018

Published in the United States of America by:
Cobb Publishing
704 E. Main St.
Charleston, AR 72933
(479) 747-8372
CobbPublishing@gmail.com
www.CobbPublishing.com

ISBN: 978-1-947622-19-7

A special thank you to all who helped me with suggestions, critiques, and encouragements throughout the creation of this book.

I couldn't have gotten to this point without you!

CHAPTER 1
Project 63X

The monster swam around in the lake for the first time. She moved up to the surface and popped her head out of the dark, green water, feeling cool air blow against the side of her fishlike head. She glanced up at the fluffy, blue clouds that swirled overhead and felt safe for once.

It had only been yesterday since she had been swimming around in a five-foot deep pool of water. For 13 years she had always lived inside the institute. She didn't even have a name, unless you think Project 63X is a name. But that's what the scientists called her.

The facility patterned a dome. On the outside it had been painted white. But, on the inside, it was the color of earwax. The halls twisted around like a long, dark labyrinth. A maze composed of many rooms with a stuffy smell, at least that's how it felt to Project 63X. To her, it seemed suffocating. She gasped for air, feeling like she couldn't breathe.

"My friends, this is Project 63X, one of my best works," announced Dr. Pold, pointing to the creature as she whirled around. "She is the key to studying water life."

Dr. Pold was a tall, middle-aged man with thinning, grey hair on top, who wore black sunglasses. He hardly ever took off his sunglasses because his eyes were sensitive. Some thought it was because of all the years that he worked under the bright lights in the laboratories.

Behind his glasses, he studied Project 63X.

A crowd of scientists sat on black seats in an auditorium, which surrounded the pool on both sides. They examined Project 63X as she sped about.

Dr. Pold presented the monster and paused. He knew that he had the scientist's attention, which was exactly what he wanted. In truth Dr. Pold loved nothing more

than to have Project 63X displayed in front of them. He hoped to manipulate them, so that they would accept his idea to start doing human experiments. Little by little he wished to brainwash them into thinking that his ideas were good for humanity, which is why he would say every now and then, "Ladies and gentlemen, with Project 63X, we shall go far in life." In Dr. Pold's mind, it was only a matter of time.

While this went on, the scientists dressed in white lab coats scribbled words down on their notepads. Project 63X frowned at them as she darted by. For years she had known no other life than this one. And if she didn't do what she was told, Dr. Pold would send electric currents into the water to shock her not enough to kill her but just enough to make her obey.

After Dr. Pold examined Project 63X, he would talk to her. But he viewed her as a specimen. So, although Dr. Pold talked to Project 63X, he only lectured her about the success she would bring to the future. He didn't really care about her. Project 63X had no understanding of love and no realization of the outside world. In her mind, she had no real purpose until the day she broke free from her cage and escaped…

CHAPTER 2
The Boy

Dark and damp, trees surrounded him on all sides. The boy fled from a real nightmare while he hurried through a forest. He paused at a small pool of water. Peering down he spotted his reflection, the reflection of a grey creature with wings on its back and dark eyes. He saw ragged, faded-out clothes. He then touched one of his pointy ears. He noticed his teeth, the sharp fangs. But he also… noticed a man in the reflection of the water.

The boy turned and stared back at a person in a white overcoat. Just as he did so, a stray of bullets came at him. One of the bullets hit his left wing, and he gasped in pain as he took off, running.

He tried to dodge everything in his path; rotten tree roots and crinkled, brown leaves. But when he glanced back, he saw the man was still close. The boy changed his course, snapping off tree limbs in a desperate attempt to dodge his aim. Then he came to a sudden halt. Just an inch from his feet was a dangerous cliff, and below it a wide, rushing river. He couldn't go back the way he came. And so, he plunged over the edge.

If not for his wings, he would have dropped like a rock. The pain in his wing throbbed, rendering him unable to fly away. He made a large splash as his body collided with the water below.

The current pushed him forward against rocks, scraping his arms and legs. He desperately gasped for air, but the water pulled him under…

When the boy awoke, he found himself lying on a bed in a small, white, bare room. The single window to freedom was far too small for him to fit through. He got up and tried the lone door which, to his dismay, was locked. Gazing around, it seemed impossible to get out of the room. Then he noticed something. The white frame around the door was thick enough to stand on. He extended his claws, climbed up the wall, and stood on top of the door frame, holding himself up. Thirty minutes went by before a woman, probably in her mid-fifties, opened the door. She placed one foot in the doorway when he leaped down, shoved her to the side, and rushed out of the room.

The boy sprinted down a polished, wooden staircase into a wide room that appeared to be the inside of a huge house. The place was not at all what he expected. He stood in an enormous living room with pine floor. Scanning the area, he spied a black, leather couch, a TV, cedar chairs, a small card table, a bookshelf, and two wide windows. There were also six other doors. He began opening the doors, discovering a kitchen, laundry room, and three bedrooms. His hand turned the knob on the sixth door when a hand seized his shoulder. It was the woman.

When the woman's hand touched his shoulder, the boy turned to jerk out of her grasp, but then he heard a noise behind him.

He turned back and stared into the open doorway. He noticed a long hallway that led outside. Blocking the way was a tall, slender, middle-aged man with grey hair. He wore tiny, round, silver spectacles. He had an expression across his face that seemed to say, "I can help."

"Are you lost?" he asked. "My name is Nigel Boots. What is your name? Are you okay?"

"No."

The boy spit one word out of his mouth, and it was barely audible. It seemed like decades since he had talked. But Nigel was determined to ask him something else. Nevertheless, the boy pushed him out of the way, and sped off, hearing the vibrations of Nigel's footsteps behind him.

"Wait, I'm the one who pulled you out of the water!"

At this revelation, the boy stopped running. He turned to face Nigel. Somehow the boy knew that he was speaking the truth.

"Would you like me to help you?" asked Nigel, extending a hand. "Please come back with me into the living room."

The boy agreed. He followed Nigel back into the living room with the woman. And they sat down on the black, leather couch together.

CHAPTER 3

Project 63X

The scientists' voices echoed across the rippling water. Project 63X's excellent hearing made the whispers sound clear and close. Most of the time scientists commented on her graceful swimming or her stunning appearance. But this time she heard a conversation that made her furious...

"So, she's an animal. Right...?"

"What else would she be?"

"Good point. She probably doesn't even have a soul."

"Yep, probably."

Project 63X stopped swimming. Her glowing eyes flared with hurt and fury. Dr. Pold frowned, giving her a shock. In pain she grasped at the metal collar around her neck as the electrical shock rushed through her body. In a few seconds, it ended. But she knew her entire body would be sore for a couple of days. She forced herself to swim once more and glared at the two scientists up above. She didn't know what a soul was, but deep down inside she felt that what they said was wrong. It became her breaking point. She was sick of this kind of life and was going to escape. But this wouldn't be her first time…

The last time Project 63X tried to escape, she was seven years old. She remembered the horrible experience. When Dr. Pold realized she was missing, he set lose Doberman Pinchers on her. Now normally Doberman Pinchers are trained to help people but not these dogs. Dr. Pold created real monsters out of them. They lumbered down the long, dim hall after her.

Although Project 63X could run, the webbing between her toes made it difficult. The dogs gained on her. But she was determined not to give up. Just feet from freedom, she slipped and fell on her stomach. A dog leaped on her back while another snatched her by the ankle with its sharp teeth. In pain she cried out. Blood gushed

from her ankle, seeping onto the floor. The dog would not let go until Dr. Pold arrived and gave the order. Project 63X remembered how upset Dr. Pold was at her attempt to flee. The scars on her ankle were still visible, even now, six years later. This attempt caused Dr. Pold to attach the metal collar to her neck. The collar not only allowed Dr. Pold to shock her when she refused to follow orders but was also a tracking devise. If she tried to escape, he could find her, unless she could destroy the remote control he always carried.

CHAPTER 4

The Boy

When the boy had calmed down, Nigel began to talk.

"Let me reintroduce myself. My name is Nigel Boots, and this is my wife, Liza. We're both English professors at the local trade school. But, before I continue on, let's start by you telling me your name."

Name? The boy rubbed his forehead and felt a bump.

"Are you alright?" asked Nigel.

The boy felt the bump on his head again and frowned.

"Are you alright?" repeated Nigel. "Can you tell me your name?"

"No. No, I can't. I can't tell you my name! I don't even remember my name! Or yesterday! Or the day before that!"

Nigel's eyes grew wide while Liza, who was sitting beside him, turned white in the face. They glanced at each other. They didn't know what to think.

"So, you're saying you can't remember anything about yourself?" said Nigel.

The boy could barely shake his head no.

"Well, you do have a nasty bump on your head," answered Nigel. "You must have hit a rock when you were in the river."

"A rock?" The boy stood in frustration. "And now I can't remember anything! I don't even know anything about myself!"

"Well, if it helps any, you're welcome to stay with us," replied Liza.

The boy scanned the woman as she said this, focusing on her appearance. She was a tall, slender woman with shoulder-length hair, which was dyed black. She wore a blue blouse with a black skirt and had glasses on. However, unlike her husband's little, round spectacles, she wore square, framed ones.

"Is there any way that you can help me?" asked the boy.

And that's when he noticed his appearance in an oval mirror, hanging on a white wall. He sprung out of a chair and rushed over to the mirror. He put his hands on it.

"Is this me?"

"Yes," answered Nigel.

"Am I supposed to look like this?"

"Well, my guess is that a scientist did this to you."

"How do you know?"

"I don't. But it is my suspicion that you were experimented on."

"What makes you think so?"

"Because of where I found you. You were about a mile away from a place called the C-Life Institute."

The boy paused for a moment and looked down. He let the words sink in.

"Wow, so what do I do now?"

"Well, you can stay here with Liza and me, and we can try to help you. Or…" He trailed off for a moment. "You can leave. But I assure you that others may not be as

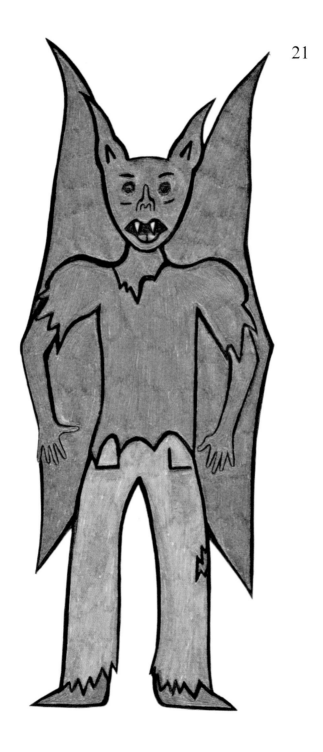

understanding as us."

The boy understood. It was because of his appearance. Others might be afraid of him, or people might try to harm him. And so, he chose to stay.

"You can sleep in the room that you were in earlier," said Nigel. "Is that okay with you?"

"Yes."

Liza and Nigel then encouraged him to go back upstairs to the room to get some rest.

CHAPTER 5

Project 63X

Project 63X waited until every scientist left, except for Dr. Pold. When Dr. Pold opened the glass door to let her out of the pool; she pushed him down before he could lay a hand on her, knocking the small, black remote control from his hand. She watched it clatter on the concrete floor, then kicked it with her wet, green foot into the pool, destroying it. White bubbles and fizz raced to the surface of the pool.

Now he couldn't track her down.

Dr. Pold scrambled to his feet to fight her but slipped over the edge of the pool and landed in the water with a big splash, spraying droplets of water everywhere. Project 63X fled. And this time as she sped through the maze of the base, there were no dogs chasing her.

She stepped through to the outside and saw that the base was surrounded by something she'd never seen before, trees. She examined the dark, looming forms that drooped in front of her, enjoying the swamp-like trees with the snaky vines that spiraled around the trunks. Nevertheless, her enjoyment didn't last long, for she feared that someone might see her. Without wasting any more time, she dashed into the woods. Hours passed by, but Project 63X was fortunate and found her desire, water. Although she had gills and air sacs, she understood she needed a safe place to hide. So, she plunged into a river and swam in the water until it poured out into an enormous lake. Although she didn't know it, the lake was known as Lake Curvation. The locals from the small town of Lulu called it that because the lake took on the shape of an arc.

Project 63X stayed in the lake and drank the water, consuming microorganisms. It was all that she needed to survive. The water was her friend and protection against the rest of the world. And during the time she spent in the lake, the water grew cold but not fro-

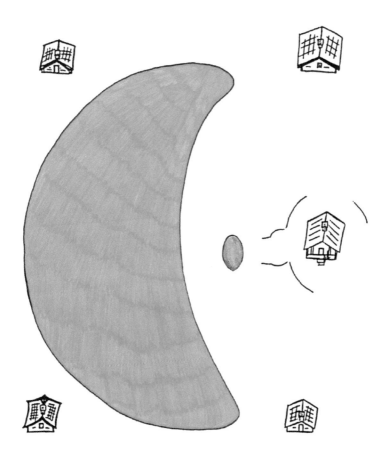

zen. She glided through the water, enjoying it, having no worries about the weather because her body temperature could adapt to hot or cold. And she would be okay.

While she traveled through the water, she perceived a layer of snow for the first time in her life. Standing on it was a boy. She had never seen a boy before and found him to be quite interesting. He was short and skinny with sandy, blond hair. His baggy, red shirt displayed the words "Nerd Power" scribbled across the front. The shirt peeked out from his poufy, unbuttoned, black coat that matched his jeans. And his black and white converse shoes were encrusted with snow.

Project 63X stared with fascination as the boy advanced onto a frozen pond 15 ft. away from the lake. She observed the way he tiptoed across the pond, which sparkled in the sun. And just as he took another step, a crack formed, splitting the ice apart. Freezing water seeped up from the thin layer of ice, and the boy dropped.

Project 63X sprinted out of the lake.

Dripping from head to foot, she crunched her webbed feet onto the snow to get to him. When she reached the edge of the pond, she dived through the break in the ice and hurried to the boy. She grabbed him by his shirt and pulled him to safety.

The boy lay sprawled on the snow, coughing and gasping for air. Project 63X stood over him to make sure that he was alright. Once he pulled himself together, he peered up at his rescuer, not in fear but in astonishment. He seemed to have no strength in him.

"Help me," he said.

"How?" answered Project 63X, replying in a cracked, whispered voice.

The boy stretched out his numb, pink hand, and she grasped it, pulling him to his feet. As he leaned against her, he pointed to a snowy hill where a small house stood with a red, shingled roof encrusted with snow and melting icicles. It was where he lived.

Project 63X paused next to a wooden rocking chair with the boy on a front porch.

The porch had been painted a pale blue, almost white. The boy opened the front door. They proceeded onto a floor and strolled through a long hallway that opened into a living room. While they traveled together, Project 63X glanced around anxiously. She did not like being in the closed space. It reminded her of the base. She wished to turn around and flee but could not bring herself to do it. She tried to follow the boy into his bedroom, but he made her wait in the hall until he changed out of his wet clothes.

He wrapped himself in a two-tone, green blanket and sat on his navy, blue bedspread and stared at his visitor.

"Are you in a costume?" he asked.

"What's a costume?"

"You're joking, right?"

The two of them stared at each other for a moment. Project 63X yearned to get out of the house and head back to the lake.

"My name is Carl Ubert," he said. "What's your name?"

"Name?"

"Yes, what's your name?"

"Well, the scientists call me Project 63X."

"You're kidding! And yet you look so real."

Carl hopped off the bed and rushed up to her. He studied her green appearance. Her head was shaped like a fish, but the rest of her body had a human form. She possessed a single fin on each arm.

Project 63X's huge, golden eyes eerily gleamed at him. While Carl strolled around her, he noticed that she wore a green, water-proof suit that matched her coloration.

"You're the real deal."

"Real deal?"

"Yes, you really are a monster.

"Yeah, so?"

Carl was alarmed by Project 63X's an-noyed reaction. He could sense that she was about to bolt.

"What's wrong?"

Project 63X started to dash out of the room. But Carl grabbed her by the arm,

holding her back.

"Wait, maybe I can help you."

"I don't need any."

"At least let me pay you back for saving my life."

Project 63X wondered how he could possibly pay her back. Even though she said nothing, Carl gestured for her to follow him. Instead of leaving the house like she wanted, he led her into the kitchen. It was a small area with beige tiling on the floor and matching, brown cabinets. There was also a little oval table in the middle of the room with two woven-back chairs. The white refrigerator and deep freezer sat in the far corner next to a black stove.

"What do you like to eat?" he asked, opening the fridge.

"Eat?"

"You do eat, don't you?

Carl searched through the refrigerator but didn't see anything good enough to eat. So, he opened the deep freezer and peered inside. His eyes landed on ice cream, cappuccino and dark chocolate, and his face broke into a large smile.

"How about ice cream?" he asked, pulling out a tub. "This is my favorite kind. Have you ever had it?"

"No."

"Well, there's a first time for everything."

Carl snatched two glass bowls out of a cabinet and grabbed two spoons. He scooped the ice cream into the bowls. It was difficult to do so because the ice cream hadn't thawed. But he managed to do it and gave one to his green visitor.

"Hope you like it," he said, wolfing his down.

At first, Project 63X was reluctant to try the solid food. But when she saw Carl eat his, she grasped the spoon, stuck it in the ice cream, and watched it sink down. Then she took a bite.

The taste was unlike anything she had ever eaten before, but she liked it and shoveled spoonful after spoonful into her mouth.

Just as she scooped up the last bite, Carl's expression suddenly changed.

"Oh wow, it's almost five thirty," he gasped, scanning his black, digital watch.

He snatched the bowl from Project 63X. He placed it down on the counter. With a gesture, he explained that his mom would be home soon.

"So, you need to get out of here," he said. "Do you understand?"

She nodded, then she hurried away from the house. She was glad to get out of that place.

CHAPTER 6

Gargoyle

Time passed while the boy stayed with Nigel and Liza, helping around. He learned quite a bit about Nigel and Liza. They were both good people who went to worship services on Sunday and tried to inspire their College students to use their talents for good. However, at the moment, they were on their Christmas break, so they spent most of their time at home with the boy working with him. They didn't mind one bit though because they didn't have any children of their own. Nigel and Liza met each other late in life. Any real family they had lived too far away, so they were thrilled to have the boy around. And the boy spent a good deal of time with them in the house, learning to improve his reading, writing, and math skills. He had some experience with math and could read and write a little. So, he did his best to improve and tried to read books that were lying around. He also practiced flying around the house, especially after his left wing got better when Nigel removed the bullet.

Nigel and Liza decided to give the boy the nickname Gargoyle, which was okay with him because it was better than being called "hey." Although this helped improve matters, Gargoyle grew restless because he stayed indoors all the time to keep people from seeing him. And now the weather had turned cold. He sprawled his legs out on the black, leather couch in the living room, trying to read a book about a couple of kids who were being chased by a monster. He didn't know if this was the way he should be spending his time. But at least the story intrigued him. And for a moment, his imagination ran away with him, but then he sat up. Something clicked in his mind. Although his life was good with Nigel and Liza, questions plagued him. Who was he? What was the purpose of his life? Did he have parents? He pressed his hands against his face. A line creased across his forehead. Nigel entered the living room and studied Gargoyle for a good, long minute. Gargoyle didn't even notice.

"Is something on your mind, Gargoyle?"

Gargoyle broke from his trance and stared up at Nigel whose eyes were full of love and compassion. Nigel's little, round spectacles sparkled from the ceiling light.

"What do you do when something bothers you?" replied Gargoyle. "Or… what do other people do?"

"Mm…, well that's a good question."

Nigel stroked his grey beard. The beard gave him a rather fairly, unique appeal. And, frankly, he looked quite good in one. His beard was now more white than grey with silver streaks. And he contained wisdom in his eyes that said more than his mouth.

"Well...," he stroked his beard again.

"Yes…?"

"Well, some people share their thoughts with others. Some people find a source of

entertainment. And some people take long strolls to get things off their minds. But as for me…"

"Yes..?"

"Well, when something is bothering me. I simply pray."

"Pray?"

"Yes, because sometimes I don't always understand and know the answers. But I know that God does. And although I may not receive an answer right away, I know that if I have faith in God, he will help me. It may not be the way I want it to be," he added quickly, "You can't always have everything you want."

"Then why bother praying at all?"

"Because God understands what I need. There is a difference between needing and wanting. If I simply ask God to make all my students smart just so that I look good as a professor, he's not going to do it."

"Why not? I think you deserve it."

"Perhaps. But, you see, I'm not asking out of love. It's true that I want my students to pass my class. But it would be far better for my students to work hard and grow spiritually as adults than to have all the answers handed to them without any effort. It would be nice if all my students were highly, gifted geniuses. But I have a feeling that God loves everyone for who they are and desires for them to learn at their own pace."

"Huh, well when you put it that way, praying doesn't seem so bad. Maybe I'll try it."

"Good. Would you like me to teach you how?"

CHAPTER 7

Project 63X

The next day Project 63X awoke to find that snow was falling. The world sparkled white as she beheld decorative, delicate flakes fall from the sky and land on the water, melting away. She loved it. But even as she watched the snow, her thoughts drifted to the boy and his unusual kindness to her. She had never met anyone like him before and wondered about the life he lived. She passed the whole day, thinking of him.

In a couple days, the sun broke through the clouds, shining out and making the air brighter and warmer. The snow had stopped, and she could spot Carl's house, sitting on the hill glazed in snow. By noon much of the snow melted into puddles of water.

Project 63X spied Carl, strolling down the hill. He stopped at the edge of the lake and stared out as if he were searching for something. Perhaps he was looking for her.

A few seconds later, she popped out of the water and headed to him. It was clear by his expression that he wasn't expecting her.

"It's you!" said Carl.

Project 63X cautiously stepped over to him. She wasn't use to one on one interaction. But since Carl had been nice to her, she wished to make friends.

"I… I just wanted to thank you for the ice cream the other day," replied Project 63X, gazing at him with her yellow eyes.

"Don't mention it," smiled Carl. "Besides I owed you big time."

Carl stared down at the ground with his hands in his pockets. He tried to think of something else to say. Project 63X watched him with interest.

"So… where are you from?" asked Carl, finding his words again.

"The C-Life Institute."

"You live there?"

"I did."

"What was it like there?"

Project 63X turned her head away and

paused, mulling over whether to say anything else about the base.

"Smelly, chemically. A bunch of scientists and not enough fresh air."

"What do you mean?"

"I mean, I was never allowed outside. Dr. Pold wouldn't let me. But that's different now…"

"Who's Dr. Pold?"

"He's the one in charge of the institute. I was his main project, which he studied all the time. He would even have me swim around in a pool for other scientists to see. And if I didn't do what I was told, he would shock me."

"Shock you?!" His eyes widened.

"Yes, with this," said Project 63X, pointing to the collar around her neck. "Dr. Pold had a remote to it, but I destroyed it."

"What does Dr. Pold look like?"

"Well, he's fairly tall, and has grey hair. And he always wears sunglasses."

"Is he married?"

"No, he never made time for a relationship. He was always too busy with his work."

"So… what happened? Did you run away?"

"Yes, and I'm not going back."

Project 63X meant it too. She planned never to go back to the C-Life Institute. If she had to, she would spend the rest of her life in hiding.

"Well, in that case," said Carl. "If you need any help, let me know."

Carl's words made Project 63X smile. And although she didn't know it, this was the beginning of a friendship. From then on, the two of them met at the edge of the lake. In return Carl took off her metal collar using his dad's copper, hand chain-cutter. He even gave her the name Zorah.

Project 63X frowned. "What did you just call me?"

"Zorah. It's a good name for you. It reminds me of a character from a game I use to play."

"Why do I need a name?"

"Because a name is how you identify yourself differently from others. It's a part of who you are. And with it, others will know who you are."

"Oh. Well, in that case, I don't mind."

"Good. Because it was cruel that Dr. Pold didn't give you a name. And Project 63X is NOT a name in my book."

In addition to giving Project 63X the name Zorah, Carl also taught her about the things of his world, like school. He told her he was in the eighth grade, and that his favorite class was Biology because he loved science. He even showed her his science project, a bug collection. It contained all kinds of insects; odd shaped beetles, peculiar wasps, and many more creepy-crawlies preserved behind a glass case.

"So, what do you like?" asked Carl.

"What do you mean?"

"I mean, what do you do?"

"Swim."

Carl set his bug collection down on the ground beside him. He tried to think of

something else to say.

"Carl," said Zorah.

"Yes."

"What's a soul?"

Zorah had been thinking about it ever since she heard those scientists talking about her back at the institute when they assumed that she didn't have a soul. For some reason, it bothered her. And she needed to talk to Carl about it. She was sure that he knew the answer.

"In what sense?" asked Carl.

"In the sense... that you... have a soul."

"Well, everybody has a soul."

"Including me?"

"Of course. A soul is the part of you that's inside. Not your physical body."

"It's inside of me."

"Yes, it's your spirit that lives inside of you that is made up of your thoughts and feelings."

Zorah pondered about this and somehow knew that Carl was right. This was what she loved about him. He always seemed to have the answers to her questions. She enjoyed his company. However, every now and then she felt distant from him.

"You sure do a lot at school," said Zorah, sitting on the grass next to the lake.

"Yes, but it's worth it," answered Carl, joining her. "When I'm done, I'm going to be a doctor."

"Really!?"

Zorah didn't know if she liked that. After all, Dr. Pold never treated her right. A frown crossed her face.

"Are you sure you want to be a doctor?"

"Sure, I love to help people. And I'm great at science. What about you?"

"What do you mean?"

"What are you going to do when you grow up?"

Zorah remained silent.

Carl suddenly blushed from ear to ear. "I'm sorry. It was a stupid question. I know you can't go to school."

"Yeah…"

"Hey, but at least we're friends. That's

got to count for something."

Noticing Zorah's confused expression, Carl explained to Zorah that they were friends because they got along with each other and spent time together.

"I guess you have friends at school," commented Zorah, looking down.

Carl's face turned a light shade of pink. Zorah was baffled. Maybe it was rude of her to ask something like that. But just the same she waited for him to answer.

"Well, the thing is…"

"Yes?"

"I spend most of my time studying at school. You see, the other kids are too busy goofing off to notice me," he said, before quickly adding, "which is fine with me because I don't mind one bit. I prefer to be alone."

"So… does that mean you don't want to be friends with me anymore?"

"No, of course not. You're different. I don't mind being friends with you."

Zorah smiled, but she got the impression that Carl wasn't telling her everything. And her look showed her suspicion.

"What?" asked Carl.

Carl felt Zorah's eyes burrow into him, and his face turned an even brighter shade of pink. He couldn't stand her stare. It only took a second before he caved in.

"Oh alright, if you must know, no one at school wants to be my friend because I'm such a nerd."

"A what?"

"A nerd. In other words, they think I'm a know-it-all because I'm pretty much good at every subject."

"And that's bad?"

"It is if people are trying to cheat off you."

"Cheat?"

Carl informed Zorah that some kids at school didn't always do their homework and tried to take the easy way out. And because he refused to let them cheat, he got made fun of a lot. Kids picked on him and called him names.

"But I try not to let it bother me. After all, they are only cheating themselves when they don't do their homework."

"Yeah and at least they can go to school."

"Yeah… Hey, wait a second!"

"What?"

"You want to learn, don't you?"

"Yes."

"Well, I've got a great idea. Why don't I teach you?"

Zorah almost fell into the lake. She wasn't so sure this was a good idea. It's not that she didn't want to learn, she just didn't have a lot of experience, and the idea made her anxious.

"Come on, it'll be fun. You'll see."

Carl dashed away before Zorah could say no. And just like that it was all settled. Carl decided that he was going to teach Zorah all the things he had learned at school. And so, every day after Carl got home from school, he spent time with her.

CHAPTER 8
Gargoyle

"Gargoyle, I need to talk to you. Do you mind?"

Liza eyed Gargoyle through her square, framed glasses. She studied him as he lounged on the black, leather couch in the living room. It was his favorite spot when he wanted to read. As tough as he looked, he seemed quite harmless when he read a book. Liza stood, waiting patiently. At last Gargoyle glanced up. He was use to her stern but caring nature. He almost broke into a smile when he realized that she was glaring at him.

"No, what's wrong."

"Nothing, it's just that I thought you should know that Nigel and I are invited to a Christmas party tonight. The other faculty members will be there as well. I needed to tell you this because…"

"Because you don't want me to go. I

know. I would just endanger my life any-way."

"Well, at least you understand. I just didn't want you to be offended. I really wish that you could go."

After Liza said this to Gargoyle, she left him alone which got Gargoyle thinking about some things. He loved living with Nigel and Liza. But at the same time, he felt as though something was off. If only he had answers. He had prayed to God and found comfort. But as time passed, Gargoyle became restless again. Perhaps if he went out into the world for a bit, he would find his calling. If he did leave, he would wait until after Christmas. It was those kinds of thoughts that caused him to fidget. And he became even more fidgety when it was time for Nigel and Liza to go to the party.

Gargoyle waved goodbye to Nigel and Liza as they left the house. As their car disappeared in the distance, he smiled. It had been a long time since he had been out.

Wasting no time, Gargoyle opened the

door and hurried out. It felt good to breathe clean air again. The cold breeze blew against him, but he didn't mind. He was just happy to be outside.

He climbed up the side of the snowy house, using his claws, even though he knew he could fly his way up. Once he was on the roof, he plopped down on the icy shingles and gazed into the night as snowflakes started to spit. He got lost in amazement, watching the flurries. But after about forty minutes, he decided that he should go back into the house. He glided to the ground when someone called out.

"You! No, don't come any closer. Whatever you are!"

He would have never known that she was there if she hadn't said something. But at the sound of her voice, he spotted a young girl, sitting underneath a tree not too far away. As he examined her, he could see she had blond hair and was about twelve or thirteen years old. He stood in front of her. When he got closer to her, he could tell that something was wrong. He had the feeling that she was lost. Despite her continuous warnings, he proceeded. Now Gargoyle was almost five feet in front of her. But that's as far as he got because she charged at him.

Gargoyle thought the girl was going to crash right into him, but she didn't. She completely vanished right through him. And as she did, he felt a wet mist. Then somehow the girl appeared on the other side of him. And without hesitation, she hopped on his back.

Gargoyle struggled to get her off. She was trying to strangle him, so he flew straight up in the air and knocked her away. He then turned back around to catch her before she fell, but the girl turned into a cloud of mist and landed on the ground. Peering down, he tried to figure out some way to get her.

Gargoyle noticed the snow was starting to come down fast and in huge clumps. He realized that the girl was shivering. Deciding that this was the moment that he had been

waiting for, he chose to try and reason with her. He landed on the ground in front of her.

He raced up to her, and again she posed to attack. He thought she would become a mist again, but she didn't. He perceived that she was trying but couldn't. Realization hit him. The cold was keeping her in a solid form. He grabbed her wrist.

"Let me go!"

He didn't loosen his grip. He wasn't trying to hurt her. Gargoyle had to make her comprehend.

"You aren't taking me. Let me go!"

"Look, I'm not going to hurt you."

But she struggled against him. At last after about a minute, he managed to drag her around the front and that was when he spotted two people he wasn't expecting to see, Nigel and Liza. Their mouths dropped open when they saw him. They both had a bundle of brown grocery bags in their arms.

"Gargoyle?" said Nigel, dumbfounded.

Nigel and Liza were speechless. But Gargoyle explained about the girl, and their expressions lightened up a bit. A second later, he opened the front door with his free hand and let Nigel and Liza enter. The girl fought against him, but he lugged her inside and shut the door. By the time he did, Nigel and Liza had dumped their bags on the floor in the hall.

"What's in the bags?" asked Gargoyle, trying to divert their attention away from the struggling girl.

"Water and food," answered Liza.

"But I thought you guys were going to the Christmas party."

"We were," she answered. "But we heard that a blizzard is going to arrive later tonight. So, we decided not to go and went to the store instead."

"Yes, and now, Gargoyle, would you please let go of that girl," replied Nigel.

Gargoyle released his hold, and the girl stopped struggling. Her face was red and puffy with anger and fear. She didn't try to run away but kept glancing around the room in confusion.

"Gargoyle, if you don't mind, I would like me and Liza to talk to this girl alone while you wait here in the hall," said Nigel. "Is that okay with you, young lady? My wife and I would like to help you?"

The girl peered up at Nigel through her watery, blue eyes. She nodded, and Liza took her by the hand, leading her into the living room. Nigel followed. After about five minutes, Nigel called Gargoyle, and he entered the living room. Gargoyle discovered Nigel, sitting on the couch alone. Liza traveled back into the hall to get the groceries.

"Gargoyle, I'm disappointed in you for taking a risk when you went outside," he said in a grave voice. "But I'm glad that you found Misty."

"Misty?"

"Yes, the girl you found. Her name is Misty Bannie."

"Where is she?"

"I sent her to the bathroom to get cleaned up. Anyway, Misty told me about why she ran away."

"She ran away?"

"Yes, and Liza and I promised her that we would do our best to help her. And I'm sure you will too."

With a small smile, Gargoyle nodded. He had no intentions of hurting anyone. After all, he was trying to make friends.

"Good, I'm glad to hear of it," said Nigel.

Nigel then lowered his voice and talked to Gargoyle about Misty. He told him about how she had lived in a children's home and why she fled using her ability. He explained that the trouble all started the day Misty had been playing hide and seek with her friends at the home. While Misty was playing, a lady named Prazel Twix caught her using her ability. Nigel admitted that he was mystified by what Misty told him, but then she demonstrated her talent for him and Liza. Then Nigel shared that Prazel Twix wanted to adopt Misty, but it was because she wanted to use her as leverage and make some money. Misty became afraid and ran away.

"Misty says that as long as she has re-membered, she has been able to transform into a cloud of mist," said Nigel. "If Prazel Twix ever finds her, I fear the worst for her. Misty needs prayers."

"Does that mean that Misty will be staying with us for a while then?" asked Gargoyle.

"Yes, if I can help it. Now, Gargoyle, I want you to get some sleep, okay?"

"Okay, Nigel."

CHAPTER 9

Zorah

At first Carl thought it would be easy to teach Zorah, but he quickly changed his mind. Zorah didn't even know how to do basic math. Years of being trapped inside the institute left her unequipped with the necessary knowledge to function in the normal world. She had never been taught math, science, history, art, or even how to write. It was Dr. Pold's wish to keep her ignorant and dependent upon him. Carl had to be patient and go at a slow pace for her. He became frustrated at times but wouldn't give up on her.

"Here."

Carl placed ten smooth pebbles in front of Zorah. He then sat on the ground next to her.

"Okay, if I have ten pebbles," he said, "and I take three away. How many do I have left?"

Zorah watched as Carl scooted three pebbles away. Yesterday he had worked with her on numbers, so today he was testing her to see what she had learned. She stared at the remaining pebbles and tried her best to count them the way Carl had taught her. Several seconds later she finally came up with an answer.

"Seven."

"Great, you're catching on!" smiled Carl, giving her two thumbs up. "Now let's practice your writing."

Carl slipped off his blue backpack and unzipped it. He pulled out a pencil and notebook, which he handed to her. Zorah took them, placing the items in her lap.

"Okay, now I want you to write your name," he said.

She opened the notebook to a clean sheet of paper. She concentrated hard but gripped the pencil in her hand and began to write. Her hand was shaky as she pressed down on the paper. But eventually she wrote out "Z-O-R-A-H" in big letters for Carl.

"Good job!"

Carl was proud of her. Zorah was making progress and that's what counted.

CHAPTER 10
Gargoyle

Misty stayed with Nigel, Liza, and Gargoyle during the two-day blizzard. Nigel and Liza talked about her. They couldn't decide whether Misty should stay with them or not. Nigel yearned to adopt her, but Liza wasn't so sure that it was a great idea. True, she wanted Misty to have a home. She just wasn't so sure this was the right environment. And Misty was still freaked out about Prazel.

"I hope Prazel doesn't find me," she replied, sitting on the black, leather couch with Gargoyle.

"Well, if she does, she'll have to face me," he answered.

"Yeah, if she saw you, maybe she'd leave me alone for good. And then I can get adopted by someone nice."

Gargoyle smiled as Misty cheered up. He almost wanted to tell her that Nigel was thinking about adopting her but decided he didn't want to raise her hopes. Besides she might not even want to live with them anyway.

"You know what's sad," said Misty, resting her head on her hands.

"What?"

"That I never even knew my parents. They died when I was six months old. I just wish I knew what they were like."

"They were probably like you."

"You think so? Are you like your parents?"

"I don't know. I don't remember. I bumped my head and can't remember."

"That's terrible!"

"Yeah, I guess it is. But then…"

"Yes?"

"But then I start to think about what Nigel says."

"What does he say?"

"Well, he says that even though he knows that his life isn't perfect, and he wants the best for those he loves, he reminds himself that imperfection is made perfect with God."

"What does that mean?"

"Well… the way I look at it is… kind of like. Well, I look like a gargoyle. And I have no memory of my past life. My life isn't perfect. And I always feel like I have to hide out. It's true that I'm an imperfect being or creation or whatever, but God can still use me."

"Yeah…, I see what you're saying. I'm an orphan, so I don't feel like I belong anywhere. I feel like I have no purpose. But God can still use me."

"Right. And I guess, to me, I'm always trying to find answers to questions that I don't truly even understand. But if I have faith and trust in God, like Nigel says, hopefully things will turn out for the best. Although… I probably should do some more praying."

"You know what?"

"What?"

"Praying sounds like a great idea. If I

start praying to God, maybe he will help me find a family. Thanks, Gargoyle. For a creature you're not such a bad guy."

"Thanks, Misty."

"No problem. But uh…"

"What?"

"Do you think you could show me how to pray? I've only seen it in the movies."

Gargoyle then did his best to demonstrate what Nigel taught him about praying. After Gargoyle and Misty said their prayers, they talked a bit more. Not long after they were done, Nigel and Liza entered the living room. They had been watching TV in the kitchen. Liza loved to watch TV while she was cooking. Nigel and Liza kept glancing at each other, waiting to spill the news.

"Well, we have something to tell you," said Liza, clasping her hands together.

"What is it?" replied Gargoyle.

"Well, it's about Misty."

"Me?"

"Yes, we were just watching the local news channel and...."

"And…"

"And I think you will be pleased to know that Prazel Twix won't be able to stalk you anymore. She has been arrested."

"Arrested?"

"Yes, she was charged with theft because she tried to steal from a pharmacy."

"She was also charged with other crimes as well, which has not been explained to the public yet," added Nigel. "But her arrest for theft was all over the news."

Misty was so overjoyed that she kept becoming a mist, disappearing and appearing. And that was when Nigel decided to ask the question.

"Would you like us to adopt you? Would you like to live here with me, Liza, and Gargoyle?"

Misty stopped changing her form. It caught her by surprise. But then she smiled.

"Yes."

"Good, then I'll take you back to the children's home tomorrow and see if I can get things straightened out."

As promised, the following day, Nigel drove Misty to the children's home. He didn't have to worry about taking off, since it was the day before Christmas. When they were gone, Liza informed Gargoyle that it would take some time before Misty could officially live with them. There would be a lot of questions, background checks, and paperwork. And then she informed him that if they're approved, there would be a good chance that it would take up to six months before Misty could live with them. To Gargoyle it sounded like a lot of work.

A Christmas meal of turkey, creamed potatoes, green bean casserole, corn, and rolls was waiting on Nigel when he returned later that evening. Gargoyle helped set the table and prepared tea for everyone to drink. It was a nice dinner. During the meal, Nigel talked with Liza about how a woman from the children's home would be sent to check them out in about three weeks. He wanted Gargoyle to hide out when the woman arrived. Which wouldn't be hard, since he figured that he would just fly around outside and come back later. He didn't share those thoughts with Nigel and Liza, though. So, when it was time for the woman to arrive, he put on a jacket, which had holes cut out in the back for his wings, and he flew outside, traveling to the park.

When he arrived at the park, he found himself enveloped by a forest. It had trails that ran through and around it. But during this time of the day, most people were at work and most children at school, so there were few people there to hike or bike. All the same he had to admit that he was taking a risk at coming to the park. It was a good way for him to stretch his wings, and he didn't get caught, at least that's what he thought. But a couple of boys, playing hooky, spotted him. And the next day, the boys started a rumor at their school about a demon haunting the park. It was the same school that Carl went to. When word of the story reached Carl's ears, he became suspicious. He was thinking about Zorah and wondered if it was possible that another creature had escaped the C-Life Institute. There was only one way to find out. After he got out of school, he decided to visit the park.

CHAPTER 11
Gargoyle and Carl

Nigel and Liza were teaching at the college when Gargoyle decided to go back to the park again. He landed on a huge oak tree, covered in brown, stringy moss and caked in old snow. While he was up there, he spotted a boy, running hard and fast down one of the hiking trails.

"Hey, Carl, where do you think you're going?" said a boy.

"Yeah, you can run, but you can't hide!" shouted another.

Gargoyle watched Carl as he fled down the trail, coming in his direction. Four boys were chasing him. It was at this moment that he decided to intervene. This kid was going to get hurt if something wasn't done. Gargoyle seized Carl and pulled him up into the tree. Carl tried to scream, but Gargoyle kept his hand over his mouth to keep him quiet.

"Don't be afraid, I'm only trying to

help."

Gargoyle took his hand away as soon as the boys were out of sight. Carl didn't say anything but just stared at him in shock. But at last he found his courage and spoke.

"Whooareyouu?" he said, slurring his words. "I mean who are you?"

"My name is Gargoyle."

When Gargoyle said it, he realized that his name wasn't going to make matters any easier. This boy must have thought he was a real gargoyle.

But Carl didn't think that way. In fact, he put one and one together and got two. Carl was convinced that Gargoyle was an experiment like Zorah.

"Are you from the institute?"

"Institute?"

"The C-Life Institute."

"What do you know about the institute?"

Carl then explained to Gargoyle about Zorah, and what he learned from her concerning Dr. Pold and the institution. In return Gargoyle enlightened Carl about how he lost his memory and was living with Nigel and Liza. This was an amazing discovery, and Carl couldn't wait to invite Gargoyle over to his house.

"Would you like to meet Zorah?"

"Yes, but I need to be getting back to Nigel and Liza. But I don't mind coming over tomorrow. Where do you live?"

CHAPTER 12

Dr. Pold

Carl opened his front door and stood face to face with a man in a black suit and white overcoat. The man's sunglasses shined in the sunlight. Carl knew exactly who it was, Dr. Pold.

"Have you seen this creature?" Dr. Pold pulled out a picture.

Carl glanced down and saw Zorah. His face turned a pale white. Dr. Pold noticed this.

"Where is she?"

"I don't know what you're talking about."

"You're lying."

Dr. Pold took a menacing step toward him. He grabbed Carl with his big, gnarly hand. Carl struggled to free himself, but Dr. Pold wouldn't let go. He pulled a needle from his lab coat and plunged it into his arm. Carl tried to jerk the needle out, but he

passed out.

Zorah watched helplessly from Lake Curvation as Carl was placed into the back of Dr. Pold's silver car and driven away. Zorah knew there was only one place that he was being taken to, the institute. She didn't want to go there, but she had to. Before she had a chance to start swimming there, she spotted two dark forms gliding down to the ground, Gargoyle and Misty. She remembered Carl explaining to her that Gargoyle was coming to visit today. When Gargoyle landed on the ground with Misty, Zorah popped out of the lake and hurried to him. Startled, Gargoyle turned and flashed his dark eyes.

"You! You're, Gargoyle, right…?"

"Yes, and you must be, Zorah."

"Please! You have to help me."

"Why? What's wrong?"

"Carl's been kidnapped. Come on!"

CHAPTER 13
Carl

Dr. Pold brought Carl to the dome-shaped base. He dragged the drugged boy through the halls. Through Carl's nightmarish, half-sleep state, the place appeared as a rundown nursing home with its long, looming halls and yellow walls. With each step that Dr. Pold took, Carl jerked from conscious to unconsciousness. His thoughts created illusions of strange, dark forms moving in and out of the walls. His eyes played tricks on him, and Carl thought he kept seeing large, grotesque rats with glaring, red eyes.

At last Dr. Pold heaved Carl into one of the lab rooms. Carl struggled to get up but was too dizzy. He could not think straight. His world was tilting and turning. Dr. Pold then stripped him of his wallet and cellphone and shoved him in a massive animal cage where Carl drifted into unconsciousness again.

Thirty minutes went by before the drug wore off. Carl jerked awake and gasped for air. Shaking all over, he grasped the cage bars. He was finally aware of his surroundings and found himself locked in a cage. Dr. Pold was nowhere in sight. Frantic, Carl tried to squeeze through the steel bars but could not. He tried to think of some other way to get out of the cage, but then Dr. Pold strolled into the room. When he noticed that Carl was awake, he loomed over the cage and peered down at Carl through his sunglasses.

"Now, are you going to tell me where she is?"

CHAPTER 14
Zorah, Gargoyle, and Misty

Zorah, Gargoyle, and Misty hid behind a maple tree and watched a scientist slide a cardkey to get into the base. Before the door shut, they rushed over and slipped inside. The scientist didn't hear them and wandered down the corridor.

Zorah took off down the hall toward Dr. Pold's personal lab and gestured for the others to follow her. Several minutes later they pushed their way into a lab room and spotted Carl in a cage. She sprinted over.

"Zorah, I'm sorry. I had no choice."

"What do you mean?"

"I… I told him. I told him about you. I'm sorry."

At first Zorah had mixed feelings. She felt a little betrayed, but then she recalled how Dr. Pold tortured her with electric shocks. She then realized that Dr. Pold had no intention of letting Carl go.

"Come on! We've got to get Carl out of this cage."

Gargoyle and Misty dashed to the cage. They knew it was locked and searched for the key. At last they found it on a lab table next to a beaker and measuring cup.

Zorah snatched the bronze key and unlocked the cage. Right when Carl got out, the lab door pushed open.

Dr. Pold's eyebrows shot up when he spotted Carl out of the cage along with Zorah, Gargoyle, and Misty. His shock lasted barely a second before a smile spread across his face. His eyes locked on Zorah and Gargoyle.

"Hello, Project 63X and… Project 62Y."

With a worried look on her face, Zorah backed up. And Gargoyle raised an eyebrow in confusion.

"What's the matter? Don't you remember your name?"

"That's not my name anymore," said Zorah.

"It is too. And if you want to live, I

suggest you come with me. You belong to me and no one else."

"No, I don't. You don't own me."

"Or me!" said Gargoyle, exposing his claws.

"Oh yes, I do. I found you both. If I hadn't taken you in, no one would have."

CHAPTER 15
Backstory

When Zorah was an infant, she had been abandoned by her mother and left near a dumpster. Dr. Pold found her and should have sent her to a good home. But instead he chose her for his experimentations. He was the one who made her different. The other members of the organization were unaware of his secret projects, since he was the leader of C-Life Institute. It was speculated that he had found Project 63X somewhere out in the Pacific. But they never suspected that she had once been a normal human being. It was a secret that Dr. Pold held on to and hoped to reveal someday to the other scientists.

As for Gargoyle, he too had once been normal. Dr. Pold found him when he was a toddler several weeks after finding Zorah. The poor kid had gotten lost in the swampy forest near the base. Dr. Pold kidnapped him. For months the disappearance of the little boy had been all over the news, but the authorities never discovered the truth.

For years Dr. Pold studied his so-called experiments, making sure that neither one of them knew about the other. Somehow Gargoyle learned about Zorah when he was just nine years old and wanted to help her escape. At the time he still looked like a normal boy and had not been transitioned into a gargoyle-like creature. But Dr. Pold stopped him. Zorah never even knew about it. In Gargoyle's rage, since he had unnatural strength due to the experimentation, he knocked Dr. Pold down. And for a time, he was free from the institute. The people that found him tried to help him and put him in special care because he grew up so isolated that he didn't know how to read, write, or do math, so they thought he was slow. Gargoyle didn't understand why he was put in a special care service, and he didn't realize that all he had to do was tell someone the truth and that would have been the end of Dr. Pold. But he didn't know that. It was like he was a wild animal. The special care director, who was an older woman, had to earn Gargoyle's trust. And for months he stayed in special care.

During the time, the director worked hard with him to figure out where Gargoyle was from. But he was so unknowledgeable that he didn't even know that he was from the institute. He did know Dr. Pold's name though but was afraid to say it. He didn't understand that the director was trying to help him and be his friend. She even tried to get Gargoyle to draw a picture of the place where he was from and placed paper and crayons in front of him. But Gargoyle had never seen crayons before and threw them at the director. It took some time to tame Gargoyle. And when he had become people friendly, the director tried again to get him to draw a picture of where he came from. With a shaky hand, he tried to draw the dome-shaped base, but it appeared more like a circle, and the director became confused.

The director then went out of her way to

help Gargoyle and worked with him, teaching him math, reading, and writing. Gargoyle caught on fast. The director decided that Gargoyle needed other kinds of help. But Dr. Pold found out where he was and came for him. Once more Gargoyle had been kidnapped, and he didn't try to escape again until six years later because Dr. Pold kept him strictly confined and bound in a small room. And it took Gargoyle that long before he got another chance to escape again. Fortunately, for Gargoyle, he remembered nothing about this.

CHAPTER 16

Facing Dr. Pold

Dr. Pold glared at Zorah and Gargoyle. To him they were his life's work. And although Zorah couldn't see his eyes, she felt like the light, reflecting off his sunglasses, was piercing her. Zorah took a step back. Dr. Pold advanced forward.

"I found you. You are mine!"

Zorah stared at Dr. Pold with horror. His words twisted something in her. A painful emotion swelled inside of Zorah, but she fought against it. Dr. Pold just smirked.

At that moment Carl spotted his cellphone on the table. He snatched it and began to dial 911. Dr. Pold's eyebrows lowered, and he charged forward to stop him, but Zorah, Gargoyle, and Misty blocked his attack. It was just enough time for Carl to get a hold of the police and give them directions.

In anger Dr. Pold jerked out a green rag and a blue bottle of chloroform from the pocket of his lab coat. He poured the color-less liquid on the rag and came at them. He was trying to knock them out. Gargoyle shoved Zorah out of the way, but he was hit full in the face with chloroform and fell over on the floor unconscious. Misty turned into a mist while Carl screamed and hopped on Dr. Pold's back, trying to knock away the chloroform. But Dr. Pold was too strong and flung Carl off his back. Misty reappeared to help Carl, leaving Zorah to face the crazed scientist.

They scuffled for a minute while Misty pulled Carl up off the floor. When Carl turned to face the doctor, he saw Zorah fall to the concrete floor unconscious. Dr. Pold then confronted Carl, but Misty got in the way. She kept fading in and out to confuse Dr. Pold. It worked for a while, but Dr. Pold snatched Carl and tossed him at Misty when she reappeared. Carl hit Misty, and she toppled over. Dr. Pold rushed up as Carl rolled out of the way. When Dr. Pold reached Misty, he used the chloroform to knock her out. Now only Carl remained to face Dr. Pold.

Carl ran at Dr. Pold and the two began to struggle with each other. Carl fought hard to keep from being knocked out and managed to smack the chloroform into the air, causing it to shatter on the ground. Pieces of broken glass flew everywhere. With a surge of anger, Dr. Pold grabbed Carl's arms and dragged him into the hall. Two policemen in blue uniforms met them in the hall. The police station wasn't far from the base, so they were able to arrive quickly. The policemen were armed and full of questions.

"We received a call about someone being kidnapped," said an officer.

"I'm afraid you're mistaken," answered Dr. Pold. "No one has been kidnapped."

Carl started to say something, but Dr. Pold silenced him with his hand.

"But we received a call," replied the other officer.

"Yes, you did," said Dr. Pold. "But not because of kidnapping. This young man

broke into the institute."

Carl protested, but Dr. Pold played inno-cent.

"No, you don't understand!" said Carl. "He's lying! He stole my wallet!"

"Is this true?" asked an officer.

"Yes, but I didn't steal it. I found it in the chemical room."

Carl could tell the policemen were be-lieving his lies. Dr. Pold had a stellar reputa-tion as a scientist, so they had no reason to believe he was making things up. Carl tried to plead his case, but they wouldn't listen. They dragged Carl away instead. As he was being pulled away, he noticed a smile form on Dr. Pold's face. Carl couldn't stand it and broke free from the officers. He jerked out his cellphone and showed it to the officers, who were shocked to find that it was the same number that had called 911. The po-licemen realized that Carl had been telling the truth and seized Dr. Pold before he could run away. While the police dragged Dr. Pold away, Carl knew there was a cold-blooded stare piercing him through those dark sunglasses. Even so, He felt a sense of relief rush over him. The villainous man had at last been captured…

News of Dr. Pold's arrest sent shockwaves through the institute, the other members were astonished that he kidnapped a boy. Many scientists left the institute in response, Dr. Pold's research was terminated, and the organization had to promote a new leader. In addition, Carl's reputation soared through the roof. A reporter came by to interview Carl at his home, and he did his best to answer the woman's questions without mentioning Zorah, Gargoyle, and Misty. Furthermore, many kids at his school now thought Carl was brave and tried to start conversations with him, instead of taunting him. As for Zorah and Gargoyle, they were both finally free from the fear of Dr. Pold. Now everything would be alright, at least that's what Zorah thought. But she also felt that there was something missing.

"What's wrong?" asked Carl.

Carl sat with his legs crossed on the ground next to the lake. Zorah was beside him, pulling out tufts of wet grass.

"Carl, I can't stay here."

"Why not?"

"Because I can't spend my whole life in a lake."

Zorah explained to Carl that she wished to help others. She told him that there could be other people out there like her who could be victims of terrible experiments.

"Then I'll go with you," said Carl.

"No, you need to stay here and finish school."

Zorah reminded him that he had responsibilities. Carl knew that she was right but didn't like to hear it.

"Then can I make a suggestion," replied Carl.

"What?"

And Carl smiled.

CHAPTER 17

The Suggestion

When Carl and Zorah knocked on the door, Liza got a surprise. She had heard so much about them from Gargoyle. In a hurry she opened the door for them to enter. But before they went in, Carl wiped his shoes off on the black and white door mat first. He was sure he had mud stuck on his shoes. As for Zorah, she more or less squished and squashed her webbed feet across the mat to get any dirt off. Once inside the house, Liza led them across the pine floor in the hall. A moment later, Nigel came rushing into the hall. Carl shook hands with Nigel and introduced Zorah.

"Sir, can I speak with you and your wife alone," said Carl.

Nigel shifted his spectacles on his nose anxiously. A second later he motioned to Liza with his hand. When Liza came over, he whispered to her. And she gave a nod of approval.

"Sure, why don't we talk here in the hall," answered Nigel. "Zorah, Gargoyle is in the living room, reading. I'm sure he will be happy to see you."

Zorah left the hall and passed through a doorway. She entered into the living room. Sure enough, Gargoyle was sprawled on a black, leather couch with a book in his hand. When he spotted Zorah, he sat up.

For several minutes Zorah and Gargoyle chatted about their recent adventures together. It was a good catch up moment until Nigel called Zorah out into the hall to talk with her. Carl took Zorah's place on the couch beside Gargoyle.

Zorah stood in the hall with Nigel. Liza had gone into the kitchen to prepare some food. Twisting her webbed hands, she stared at Nigel and waited for him to speak. He pushed his spectacles up on his nose and straightened them. He then cleared his voice.

"Zorah, I was talking with Carl about you. He wants you stay with me and Liza."

"Yes, I know. He didn't like it when I told him that I wanted to leave."

"Yes, he said that you've been living in Lake Curvation."

"Yes, that's right."

"I see… Well, would you like to live here with me, Liza, and Gargoyle?"

Zorah thought for a moment. She liked the idea of living with Nigel, Liza, and Gargoyle. But was this what she wanted? True, she didn't want to live in a lake for the rest of her life but was living with Nigel and Liza any better? And then there was Carl… He was hoping to see her again.

"If you lived here, we could help you with your education," said Nigel. "And you wouldn't have to worry about clothing or food. Wouldn't that be nice?"

Nigel and Zorah talked it over. In doing so Nigel learned a lot about her. He learned about her past and what Carl had done for her. She even explained to him that she wanted to help others.

"I think the fact that you want to help

others is good," said Nigel. "And I'm willing to help you out. But it's entirely up to you."

And that's when Zorah made a decision. She wanted a real home and a family. And she wanted to improve her education, even though she realized she would never be able to go to a real school. So, Zorah decided to stay.

CHAPTER 18
A Home

Zorah found Carl sitting at a wooden card table in the living room with Gargoyle. They had drug it out to play a game. But instead of cards on the table, there was a game of checkers set up. It was Carl's idea. Gargoyle had never played before, and Carl, for sure, knew that Zorah hadn't either. Carl then pulled up two cedar chairs for him and Gargoyle to sit in.

"Okay, I'll be red, and you can be black," said Carl, sitting down in front of the table.

When Gargoyle sat down in the other chair, Carl explained the rules. After detailing them, perhaps a little too much, they started their first game, while Zorah watched.

Carl made his first move, and Gargoyle hesitated because he couldn't tell if this was a bad or good move. It wasn't until about Carl's sixth move that Gargoyle realized that he was getting trapped as he watched his pieces become captured. Soon after, Carl seized four more of his checker pieces. Frustrated Gargoyle wondered where he could move one of his next pieces, so that it wouldn't get jumped. But everywhere he looked, he found that his pieces were going to get jumped no matter what. And that's when Gargoyle understood that the game was over, and he let Carl take his pieces.

Although Gargoyle lost, he enjoyed the game and wanted to play another round. But Nigel and Liza entered the room, so he changed his mind. Liza was carrying a plate full of warm chocolate chip cookies, which everyone dug into.

While they munched on their cookies, Carl learned a lot about Nigel and Liza and was glad that Zorah would be in good hands. It was a nice visit. And before Carl knew it, it was time for him to go home. He didn't mind one bit though because it was clear to him that Zorah would be alright and not just her but Gargoyle too. He felt that both Zorah and Gargoyle now had what they needed all along, a home and a family.

THE END

Made in the USA
Monee, IL
15 March 2020